JOURNEY INSIDE SUPERSTAR PLANET #1

THE WRATH OF MOGWAI

Written by
Sarah Amelia Tse
Illustrations by
Edward Kwok

ISBN-13: 978-0996332903
ISBN-10: 0996332901
Story by Sarah Tse
Illustrations by Edward Kwok
Book layout by D. Bass.

For Dad, Mom, Jeremy, Lolo, Lola, Grandma, Uncle Eddie,
Uncle Rich, Uncle Kong, Uncle Sunny and my family & friends
who influenced me and inspired me to write this story.

For all my teachers who motivated
and encouraged me especially:

J. Sigismondi, R.Hayes, H.Sucher, M. Altimari, L.Jordan,
Corinne Sandusky, Shoshanna Spector, M.Myers

When 11-year old Angela Ferrari learns that her father has been trapped inside the book, Superstar Planet, she recruits her 8-year old sister Natalie and her 14 year old brother Cosmo to try and rescue their dad.

Will Angela, her siblings and mother be able to find Mr. Ferrari and defeat the evil Mogwai?

CHAPTER 1: JUST BEING ANGELA

Angela Ferrari was a normal, average 11-year old. She lived in a house in Brooklyn, New York, with her 8-year old sister Natalie, 14-year old brother Cosmo and her mother Sandra.

Angela was always curious about her father. Since her father left the family when Angela was only 3, she didn't even remember who he was. Her mother told her his name is Franklin. Everybody called him Frank.

There was this odd book on Angela's bookshelf that she was interested in reading. It was known as The Chronicles of Superstar Planet. She never considered it to be just a "book," because whenever she got to the end of this particular book, more pages always seemed to magically appear. Although it was quite strange, Angela loved reading it.

One rainy night, Angela heard voices in the hallway. It was her mom, Sandra, talking to someone. It was a teenage girl with a little boy. Angela was supposed to be fast asleep, but she was too curious. Determined to know what was going on, Angela opened the door until it was ajar. She heard the teenage girl say,

"I'm Sarah Infinite Star. This is my little brother, FireJeremy. We're here from Superstar Planet."

"They're aliens", thought Angela, who was trying to keep quiet, when she stepped on something painful. "Ouch!" she exclaimed.

Suddenly, Sandra turned around and said, "Angela, why are you still awake?" Shyly, Angela showed her face.

Sandra then turned around and said, "Sarah Infinite Star and FireJeremy, this is my nosy daughter Angela. She is 11 years old. I also have a 14 year old son and an 8 year old daughter."

"Hello!" FireJeremy exclaimed.

"Uh, hi," Angela replied, smiling a bit. "Where's this place… Superstar Planet," asked Angela, "and how do we get there?"

"There are two ways for the Earth people to enter Superstar Planet," Sarah Infinite Star replied. "One is to read the book, The Chronicles of Superstar Planet, and two is to find a secret portal. The secret portal is hidden in the weirdest places."

"Is Superstar Planet very far away?" asked Angela.

"If you are wondering where it is, it's above Earth. You just don't see it because it's protected by a force field that makes the planet seem invisible."

"Are you an alien?" Angela asked,

"Well, sort of. But don't worry, we're harmless. We are just here to warn Sandra that Black Widow's son, Mogwai, is entering this planet to kill her. Mogwai is the one who captured your Dad, Franklin. Since then, Franklin has been blind for such a long time," Sarah Infinite Star explained. "We know the words you speak because our Superstar Planet is basically Earth's twin, both in life and in looks. The only difference is that superheroes and other super naturals really do exist there."

Hearing this, Angela's heart sank. She thought to herself, Could this be why my Dad is missing all this time? Why didn't mom tell me?

Eager, Angela said, "mother, can we go stop the 'Mogwai?' I promise…I can save him. I know what it takes!"

"Kids," mumbled Sandra, with a staggered laugh. "Maybe you should go to sleep. You've stayed up way too late enough reading; we can discuss this in the morning. You have seen enough."

Angela nodded and went back into her room. The door was still ajar. Angela was trying to sleep, but she just couldn't. She was too curious and too distracted, and her mind was racing.

Meanwhile, still in the hallway, Sandra said, "Thanks for warning me, Sarah Infinite Star. I will get the kids away from here." Just then, Sarah Infinite Star was gone, along with Fire-

Jeremy.

"Mom," said Angela through the cracked bedroom door, "What? Was that a warning?"

Sandra shrugged her shoulders and just chuckled to herself. "This is getting very interesting."

CHAPTER 2: FLYING OUT OF BOOKS

Wake up, Angela!" Natalie shouted at her sister with a shriek and a girlish voice, "Mama wants us to pack our bags. We're going on a vacation!" Groggily, Angela woke up.

"What? When? Huh? What about Super Star Planet?" Angela asked.

Natalie looked puzzled and said, "What are you talking about."

Angela was thinking to herself, "Was that a dream? Did I just say that?"

"When and where are we going on this vacation?"

"Now! We are going right now!" Natalie exclaimed. Angela gasped and jumped out of her bed.

"Hey, bookworm!" Cosmo exclaimed, poking Angela's shoulder, "You don't need to bring all those books! It's not a 'book club' vacation!" Angela rolled her eyes at her Big Brother.

"So? Aren't you bringing your 3DS XL and your 6 video games?" she replied.

"Uh, yeah," Cosmo said, as he walked away. "At least I'm not so obsessed with reading like you, or in love with looking cool, like Natalie,"

Meanwhile, Sandra was downstairs reading The Chronicles of Superstar Planet book in the kitchen. She was reading a couple of characters' names out loud when suddenly these figures popped out of the book. To Sandra's shock, the figures came to life! "I have a little situation here!" Sandra called out.

Sandra was attempting to close the book, but the book was trying to remain open. It was as if magic was keeping it open and swirling all over the room.

"Are you trying to close the book on us? Let us help," came from the voice of a teenage girl with a doll like face half covered with black silky hair standing in the middle of the kitchen. The girl gently closed the book with success and wasn't even stressed.

"How is it so easy for you?" Sandra asked.

"That's because I come from Superstar Planet. That is my home," the girl replied.

Angela, Cosmo and Natalie were curious about what was going on in the kitchen. They found Sarah Infinite Star and a bunch of people. "Who are they?" Angela asked.

"I forgot to introduce my friends," Sarah Infinite Star replied. "This is FireJeremy, Emily Thunder, Leannabelle, Duke, Cragger, Turtle Z, Super April, Lady Jane, Jon Jon, Allie, and Jaimie."

Sarah Infinite Star's friends were dumbfounded by the looks of the kitchen room. It was so pretty! Even Jaimie, the Goth girl of the group, smiled wide and said, "Humph, I guess this place is better than what I expected."

"It sure is! I LOVE the cute bouquet in the corner!" added Super April, referring to Sandra's flower bouquet on the counter.

6

Allie, the studious one of the group, was looking at Angela's bedroom. It was full of books. "How many books do you have?" she asked.

Angela replied, "I have 90 books and still counting. Including the stories I have written in composition notebooks." Angela smiled. Allie nodded.

"Wow! These stories are cool!" Allie exclaimed. "May I have a copy? I would love to publish them in my planet."

Angela nodded and handed over a copy. "It's a bit dusty, though. I hadn't written stories for a while due to junior high and other school things," Angela replied, "but I'm sure your customers will love — wait, WHAT?! You're a publisher? Aren't you a bit young to have a job?"

Allie replied, "According to your world, yes, but in our world, no. Anyone ranged from ages 6 to 48 can work. You work for any number of years, but by the time you're 60, you retire."

Angela said, "Interesting!"

"Angela!" someone shouted. It was Sandra, who was with Sarah Infinite Star. Sarah Infinite Star was holding Natalie's hand, and they were talking to each other.

"Yes, mother?" Angela replied.

"Come downstairs for breakfast, we're leaving soon!" Sandra shouted.

"Coming!" Angela exclaimed, and ran downstairs, leaving Allie and the 2 other girls in her room.

After eating Cheerios, strawberry milk and blueberry pancakes with bacon and feeling excited, knowing that there were magical people in her house, Angela ran back upstairs.

"Where is my Chronicles book, Mom?" asked Angela. "I don't see it anywhere."

"This kitchen is so crowded with magical people in here!" replied Sandra. "No worries, I found it under Jon Jon's feet resting on it!"

Jon Jon was sitting on the kitchen chair with his feet propped up on top of the kitchen table, on top of the book.

"Is he wearing a cape? An actual superhero cape?" thought Angela.

Sarah Infinite Star suddenly jumped up and shouted, "Into adventure!" With her wizardry wand she put it on the page. The wand created a spark and a portal expanded out, teleporting herself, FireJeremy, and the Ferraris into the small secret portal.

CHAPTER 3: HIDING FROM MOGWAI

The secret hideout/portal delivered them to a space home that was not on Earth. It is as if they were inside a spaceship, the home felt futuristic and spacey. Everywhere you looked there were electronic lights, holograms popping up everywhere, and even little robots bouncing around at your feet.

"This is a wonderful place! I also see - OMG! Are those books? And makeup sets?!" Natalie exclaimed, running over to look at a bright makeup set. "I wanna look great for this adventure!"

Whoever owned this place had everything the Ferrari children wanted. This person even knew what they loved to eat. Suddenly, an elderly man named Merlin appeared with a young woman and a little girl.

"Hello, Sarah Infinite Star!" the elderly man said.

"Who are they?" whispered the little girl.

"Oh, Lydia, ask Sarah Infinite Star." replied the young woman.

"Sarah Infinite Star, it looks like you met some new friends. Who are they?" asked Lydia, the little girl.

"This is Cosmo, Angela and Natalie," Sarah Infinite Star replied. The Ferraris' waved.

"Oh no! My crystal ball says the Mogwai is nearby! He might find us. Quick! Hide! In the closet, children! I will take care of him!" Merlin, the elderly man shouted.

"Who's Mogwai?" Cosmo and Natalie asked.

"I'll tell you later. Quick! Hide," Merlin replied, and with the wave of his hand, opened a robotic closet. They stared at him in confusion and in curiosity.

"Shush, children," Sandra whispered from the closet. The kids nodded, and kept quiet.

Mogwai entered the planet home. "Hello, Merlin and Mrs. Guide. Where is your daughter?" he asked, deeply and mysteriously.

"Lydia isn't our daughter. She's my niece and is playing somewhere in the west wing of the home," Mrs. Guide, the young woman replied.

Mogwai interrupted abruptly. "I have Franklin Ferrari as my captive. If you want to know where he is, enter my world, in exchange for the children. I know they are here. I sense them. Let me know if you made your decision."

As soon as he left, Merlin waved the closet door open. "You can come out now," he said.

Curiously, Angela and Natalie exited the closet. Cosmo exited too, but gave Merlin a look of confusion. "Why, Merlin? Why are we hiding?" Cosmo asked.

"As you heard," Merlin replied, "the Mogwai wants to capture you and your family in exchange for Franklin Ferrari, your father."

Merlin added, "I think I first found him inside Superstar Planet after flying through a portal or something. But here's the thing. He was weakened. I healed him, but by the time he thanked me, he was gone. I wonder what the Mogwai wants from the Ferrari family."

Angela was the most curious of all. She's read books before about children looking for their missing parents, and written stories about a mother looking for her missing husband.

"Who's Franklin?" Cosmo asked.

"Oh, Cosmo. That was your father, remember Frank?" Sandra replied.

Cosmo shook his head. He doesn't remember his father.

"Tell us what happened to our father!" Natalie and Angela both exclaimed in excitement. Sandra sighed and sat everyone down to tell them the story.

"So many years ago, when Natalie was a baby and Angela was only 3, I gave you a special book that has magical powers that can take you to other worlds like this one."

"Who gave you this book? Was this book the Chronicles of Superstar Planet?" Sandra just winked and smiled at her children. *"My dad gave it to me."*

The children looked at Merlin with astonishment and said altogether, "are you our grandfather?" With a warm smile, Merlin acknowledged them.

Sandra then said, *"One night when I was reading aloud from the book to get you guys to fall asleep. Franklin, your dad, was holding Natalie in his arms, and as I flipped a page, Franklin was gone. He disappeared. I looked everywhere for him, but he wasn't there. I kept flipping through pages and found a man who looked JUST like him in one of the chapters. The book said Franklin fell onto one of the pages, and was kidnapped by Mogwai, who is Merlin's evil brother.*

Angela and Natalie stared at me as if I did something wrong. Cosmo looked bored. I suddenly felt a little guilty. "Why did I ever read this book?" continued Sandra. "Was it magic? Or am I magic? I was filled with questions, so I ran over, and read the book silently in a different room to see if the magic was in me. Turns out, I am magic. Characters can fall in and out of this book when I read it."

Angela smiled wide and so did Natalie. Merlin then said, "Yes, daughter. It's a part of you, too. Magic."

"What a story! That was so... Thrilling! You know what I mean? I was always wondering about my father my whole life!" Angela thought about the story for a moment, then suddenly exclaimed, "So that's why the book seems to grow pages ever since it first appeared! The pages never end, it keeps adding on! Like magic!"

"Bravo!" Angela added, as if she just watched an opera.

"Children!" Merlin called. Cosmo, Angela and Natalie ran over to him. "I've got a present for all of you grandchildren," Merlin said, and guided them to another room.

CHAPTER 4: ARMORED WITH WEAPONS

"Wow," Natalie said in awe, "this place is amazing!"

"It sure is," Angela added, "I wish I had a place like this back at home, it looks SO amazing!" Merlin and Cosmo nodded.

"This is where I will armor the three of you," Merlin explained. "Since the Mogwai is coming to take you and your mother, you all must be prepared.

"Let's get prepared!" Merlin boomed, and snapped his fingers. Sarah Infinite Star and FireJeremy walked over to him, smiling, and handed Merlin some shiny armor, with durable weapons.

"Cosmo, since you're the oldest of the Ferraris, you will get a diamond helmet with iron armor. You will be armed with a diamond axe and a powerful dagger with a time bomb. Be sure to use the bomb wisely. I recommend using it as soon as Mogwai is destroyed. For Angela, she will be an archer with the ability to have one hundred arrows and a powerful bow. She will also have an iron helmet and magical, winged unbreakable golden boots that will allow her to levitate. As for Natalie, since she is a little bit too young to fight, I shall give her a pack of potions and some ingredients. She will also have a magical wand just like Lydia. She will be a wizard in training and will have the ability to heal injured people if she can master the potion," Merlin explained.

The children were amazed at the armor they were given. "Remember, these are powerful weapons, so try not to use them unless needed," added Merlin.

"Let's go back and show everyone our new armor," Natalie suggested. Cosmo and Angela agreed and proceeded to the room where the rest of them were.

CHAPTER 5: KIDNAPPING

Angela was fast asleep with Natalie and Cosmo. Everyone was sleeping except Sandra, who was reading The Chronicles of Superstar Planet. There was a tiny nightlight next to her, and she skimmed through each page. Suddenly, she felt like more and more pages were forming.

"What the heck?" Sandra whispered to herself. She kept skimming through the pages and found the words on the new pages of the book: Angela, Cosmo, Natalie and Sandra. Was Sandra meant to be in the stories? Was Merlin summoning more pages to the book? Was it actually unfinished?

Sandra, frustrated and confused, shut the book. Suddenly, a little magpie bird flew into the house making an eerie noise. Someone must have just forgotten to close the window, thought Sandra.

The magpie bird changed its shape into a young, dark haired woman. She had brown eyes, and wore a dark purple dress with black feathers all over it. She wore a green headband that stuck out prickly poisonous thorns, crimson-red lipstick and black onyx eye shadow.

"Hello," the woman chirped, "I'm Black Widow. My son the Mogwai was expecting you. Do you have the book?" Sandra nervously shivered and said no. "Do you speak of the truth?" Black Widow said with a threatening eye. "Don't lie."

"No, ma'am. I am not lying. What book are you talking about?" Sandra quickly responded.

"Mogwai is looking everywhere for it, and you have it. He wants the book for himself. You won't know what will happen to you after that," Black Widow explained with an evil smile. She snapped her fingers and a bony bird appeared. "Bring her to my son's palace," Black Widow commanded.

"You can't take me!" Sandra screeched, and fought to escape, but by the time she was almost out, she was flying. The bony bird must have started its flight when she started fighting. He wrapped his talons around her tightly and disappeared into the foggy night.

Angela woke up. "Merlin," she whispered, "I'm thirsty. May I get a glass of water?" Merlin, who was still sleeping, woke up and magically made a glass of water appear.

Angela ran into the living room and found the book of chronicles, drinking her glass of water. Suddenly, she heard a shriek that was coming from Sandra at a distance. "Mother!" she whispered, "Where the heck are you?" Looking everywhere, Angela was worried that her mother was gone, like her father.

"Mother! Where are you going?" she said aloud. Sandra wasn't answering. She was too high up. Angela watched her mother soar away with the creepy, bony birds. "YOU CAN'T TAKE HER AWAY!" Angela screamed.

Angela ran into her mother's room and picked up the book The Chronicles of Superstar Planet. She went back into her room and started reading, hoping for some answers. After a few minutes of reading, she shut the book and prayed for her mother to come back. She thought of her mother, and couldn't live without her. She can't imagine her mom being a slave of the Mogwai.

"Don't worry about your mother, Angela. Worry about yourself," a voice said to her, "your mother will be fine, and I believe it."

It was as if the book was talking to her.

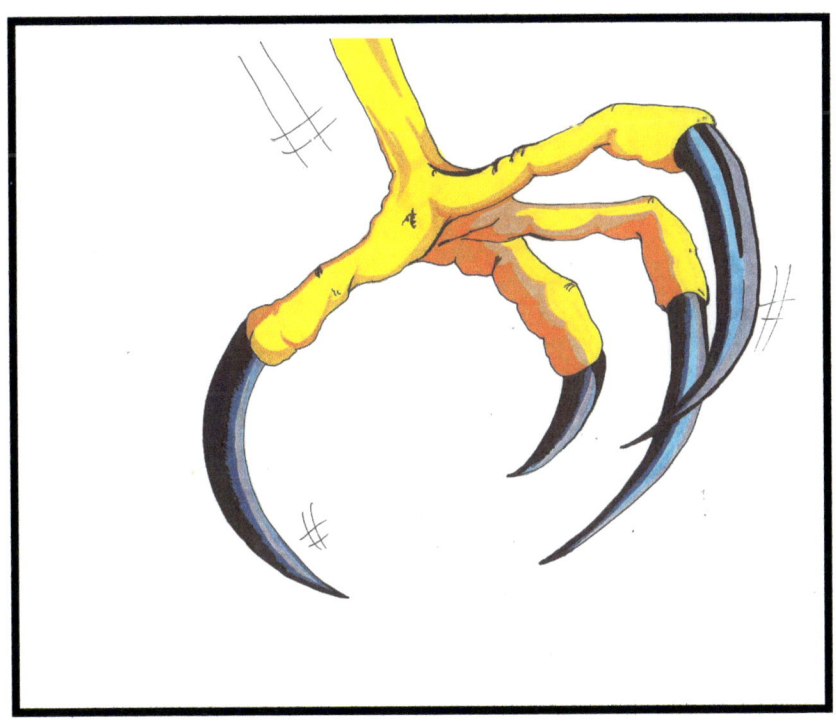

CHAPTER 6: HIDING EVEN HARDER

Merlin, why do we have to be even quieter?" asked a curious Angela when she woke up and got some breakfast, "Isn't this place quiet enough?" Merlin shook his head.

"We are being EXREMELY quiet because the Mogwai is still able to find us and Black Widow has already kidnapped Sandra," Merlin replied. He used his magic wand to lock all doors and shut all windows.

"Don't worry, Angela," Sarah Infinite Star added, "this place will still be a nice, beautiful luxury home, but you'd have to stay even quieter." FireJeremy nodded in agreement. Angela smiled in relief. "Thank God!" she exclaimed, but then she was shushed by Merlin.

He nodded. "Yes, but we must act quickly. We do not want Mogwai coming in here looking for the book," Merlin replied. Mrs. Guide nodded.

"Ready for this place to be in silent mode?" Merlin asked. Everyone nodded, and POOF! Everything seemed to be snug and secure. Radios, televisions and other loud devices were muted. Doors, windows, and machines were either closed down or slammed shut. The house alarm was set to panic mode just in case someone suspicious came inside. It also turned into a spaceship.

Luckily, Merlin created a new room, and as soon as the Ferraris entered it they fell in love with the new room.

The "room" was like a tropical resort, but everything was at low volume and it was quiet. There were a certain few rules in the room, and some of them, to Cosmo, sounded a bit stupid.

"Why do we have to be quiet? It's PARADISE!" Natalie whispered loudly.

"Because Mogwai is still looking for the book, we need to be quiet. We are hiding," Mrs. Guide replied quietly. Unhappy that they had to remain silent, the Ferraris stormed away.

We're going to have a swim," Angela said angrily and quietly. Mrs. Guide shrugged.

As the Ferraris took their swim, there was a robotic lifeguard on duty, and there was a sign that said:

Remain quiet or face the punishments!

"Seriously?" said Cosmo, "it's a luxurious place. Why are we expected to be quiet?" A statue moved and scowled down at him, saying, "To avoid the Mogwai." It soon disappeared, and Cosmo looked as if he just saw a creepy ghost.

CHAPTER 7: STOLEN IN THE NIGHT

Midnight struck again. Natalie, Angela and Cosmo and everyone else stayed up late swimming in the pools quietly. They all took a lovely splash in spite of their worries for their mom. Suddenly, along the side of the far end of the pool, a creepy looking male statue started to move. It spun an ice spell freezing the water, and everyone started to freeze, too. They were all shocked. The shadowy statue collected the children all in a net. The panic alarm went off, crazily. The figure laughed, "ha ha ha!" Mogwai laughed "I captured you!"

Angela slowly awoke and felt funny. The frozen spell was slowly wearing off. She started to get up, but the cold made her stumble. "Ouch!" she screeched.

When she got up, snow crystals were melting around her, and underneath were soil and pebbles surrounding her. *Where am I? What just happened? Why do I feel like I froze for a day?* Thoughts kept lurking in Angela's head. "AAUGH!" she screamed again. Angela jerked back hitting a wall. She looked over at her hands, and found chains on her wrists. "Oh no," Angela muttered to herself, "I am chained. Kidnapped! In a rocky dungeon! Where are Natalie and Cosmo?"

Natalie was scared. She had just discovered she was chained, and she noticed Cosmo was even more frightened than herself.

"I must learn to set myself free!" Natalie exclaimed, but how? Suddenly, there was a magic in her that told her to burn the chains, using her magic. *C'mon, Natalie. It's the only way. Burn the chains!* Voices inside her head felt like a God whispering to her ears.

Natalie commanded the works with her magic:

"Oh, pain I feel!

It irritates me, and makes me feel as if my skin will peel!

O' Fire Wizard, please burn

The chains, just turn

To them and whisper the chains to stop

And for them to pop!"

Instantly, the chains started burning. Natalie felt crisp fire attacking the chains and suddenly stopping after the chains turned into ashes. She unlocked the dungeon door, and happily exited.

Cosmo was cold and freezing. Suddenly, he felt like he had chains on his arms. "Oof!" Cosmo exclaimed, feeling both scared and cold. He felt pebbles covering his feet. He shook stones away from his feet and looked at his sister with panic at his dungeon door.

"Don't worry, big brother," Natalie said quietly, "I can free you like I freed Angela, Sarah Infinite Star, and FireJeremy."

Cosmo was shocked. It has been a while since Natalie called him "big brother." The last time he heard those words was from Natalie, when she was only 5. Memories...

"How can you do that?" Cosmo demanded.

"I don't know how, but it seems to work!" exclaimed Natalie.

The cage door was open. "C'mon, Cosmo! We have to destroy the Mogwai to get out of here!" Natalie exclaimed. Cosmo got up with a burst of energy and ran off, and together they stormed the Mogwai's castle.

"Here are the prisoners. Bring me Sandra and Franklin!" exclaimed Mogwai.

Nervously, Sandra and Franklin walked over to the Mogwai. "Welcome, Mr. and Mrs. Ferrari. We have your children. Is that true?" Mogwai asked with a threatening voice.

Sandra shook her head. "I don't know," she said.

"WHAT DID YOU SAY?!" the Mogwai replied fiercely.

"I don't know!"Sandra answered a bit louder.

"EXCUSE ME! SPEAK A LITTLE LOUDER OR ELSE MOTHER WILL CHOP BOTH YOUR HEADS OFF!" Mogwai shouted so loud that everyone started to jump.

"I'm sorry, sir. I said, 'I DON'T KNOW!'" Sandra shouted so hard Franklin covered his ears.

"Why don't you know?" Mogwai asked.

"Since YOU kidnapped me, I hadn't heard ANYTHING else about my poor children!" Sandra snapped.

"No need to shout, Mrs. Ferrari, all I want is the Book." Mogwai replied.

Sandra said, "I don't know what "book" you are talking about!"

Mogwai demanded, "MOTHER! BRING ME THE CHILDREN!" Black Widow nodded and clapped her hands. Sandra stared in horror when she found her own children, kidnapped too!

"You, too?" Sandra exclaimed. "Oh, no!"

Angela nodded, and shouted at their captor, "YOU! You are the Evil! I know EVERYTHING about you! Let us go!"

Mogwai shook his head. "No little girl shouts at an adult like that."

Angela was speechless, but she stared at him in anger.

"Shut up!" Sandra screamed, "You don't talk to my daughter like that!"

"I read about you!" shouted Angela. "You're infamous or something. I'm not just any little girl!"

Mogwai simply smirked. "I want MY BOOK!" he said. He clapped his hands. He then said, "Someone has to bring MY book or be punished!" "YOU WILL FEEL MY PAIN!"

CHAPTER 8: FRANKLIN IS BLIND

Franklin turned around and touched Sandra on the arm. "Sandra?" he asked, "Is that you?"

Sandra turned around. "FRANKLIN!" she exclaimed and hugged and kissed him. "Oh, how I missed you!"

"Mom! Why are you hugging that man?" Natalie asked dumbly. "Is that DAD?"

Franklin touched Natalie and Angela. "Why is Natalie not so small anymore?" Franklin asked. 'Why do I feel Angela is a big girl? How did my kids grow up so fast?"

Angela shrugged. She noticed he had a cane and he had black sunglasses. Whispering to Sandra's ear, she said, "is Dad blind?"

Indeed, he was blind. "Yes, I am blind, if you are wondering, child," Franklin replied. "I lost my sight when Mogwai captured me. He froze my eyes with his icy breath and made sure I couldn't see light forever."

Angela and Natalie stood there, staring at Franklin, giving

him weird looks like, *I was waiting for so many years to meet you, dad, but only to find out you're a blind, but there is this connection.*

"It's okay, girls. Take me home, and I won't be blind anymore," Franklin said, attempting to touch Angela's shoulder. Angela smiled wide and nodded. "Just be happy we're reunited again. "

"I don't like happiness!" boomed Mogwai. "Now shut up and sit down. I will speak to the old man."

Merlin stood up. "Mogwai, you used to be a good boy when you were a child. What turned you evil?" In a quiet voice he added, " I'll soon make sure you remain a good man."

Bursting out in laughter, Mogwai shouted, "Me! A good man! Ever since we were young old brother, you were always the favorite one! Old people are so funny. That ends today! You may have lived since the beginning of this planet, but I have ENOUGH of your nonsense. Hasta la vista!"

Magic swished in and attacked Merlin, but unlike elderly people, he struck back. Mogwai fell back in his throne. He placed dark magic on Sandra instead. He created a portal vortex with wind swirling all around. Sandra suddenly was lifted up and swirled up toward the portal hole.

Screaming, Natalie shouted:

Protect me, light magic!

Make enemy's powers so tragic!

Mogwai's powers bounced back and hit the wall, causing it to break, "I declare war!" Mogwai exclaimed. Sandra was sucked into the portal and disappeared. "If she doesn't have my book, then she doesn't belong here!" Mogwai then summoned the surrounding frozen statues to awake, and ordered his soldiers to attack...

CHAPTER 9: BINDING THE BOOK AND THE GREAT WAR

FireJeremy jumped off and attacked the first two soldiers, using both magic and combat. "Children! Attack! Angela, you're our only hope! Use the source of this book!" Merlin ordered.

Lydia, Sarah Infinite Star, and their friends jumped out and attacked. More soldiers started attacking, including Black Widow.

Mogwai stayed still. "Little miss Angela Ferrari. Are you going to read to me?" he asked, gently.

Confident and brave, Angela said, "I have the Book. It's an enchanting story, and I shall start."

She turned to page 38, *The Powers of Miss Lydiana*, and read:

"Lydiana was the niece of Mrs. Guide. She prefers to be called Lydia. She is powerful for her age, and now to shout a command, I shall make her shout those words!"

Lydia took the book and shouted in a command:

Thou' who hath kidnapped Mr. and Mrs. Ferrari shalt faceth punishments!

There was a silence as Mogwai turned and looked at everyone.

"This usually works!" exclaimed Lydia. "This is not right. My powers are not working!"

Angela then took her crossbow given by Merlin and shot an arrow at Mogwai. That one arrow exploded to a hundred, and showered Mogwai, who blasted a large fireball and burned all of it away.

Cosmo desperately grabbed his diamond axe and instead of trying to strike Mogwai, who was too powerful, he saw the book in a golden glow. *'What if I strike and destroy what Mogwai wants'*, thought Cosmo. He raised his diamond axe, and tried to strike the book in the center, but before he could strike it, Angela stopped him. "Wait! We all should touch the axe, together, to combine our powers!" exclaimed Angela.

Mogwai just wickedly laughed at their attempts.

"Yes! We will join together, and I will shout: *Home is where the heart is! It's where I belong. Take me and my family there, as our journey is over!*"

Suddenly, a large beam of light came out of the book. Mogwai then yelled, "At last! The answer to the universe. My access to Superstar Planet Secrets has been opened for me."

The children grabbed the axe in unity and struck the axe into the center of the book. In a flash of red and gold, Mogwai evaporated and was sucked into the book, where he was trapped. Forever.

The children released the handle, leaving the axe in the book. Looking around, the portal vortex was still there, and the other end was Earth. "Let's go back! This is our way home!" exclaimed Angela.

Cosmo remembered to set his time bomb in order to seal off the book and destroy the Mogwai in it.

"May I join, too?" asked Franklin.

"Dad! You can see! How'd it happen?" exclaimed Natalie.

"It seems that when you struck the book with your axe and trapped Mogwai inside, his spell on me broke," explained Franklin. Together, they all walked in towards the vortex, and said their final goodbyes to Merlin, Mrs. Guide, Lydia, Sarah Infinite Star and FireJeremy, leaving them back in Superstar Planet.

The time bomb exploded when they arrived at the other side of the portal, Earth.

Back at home, Sandra was in her kitchen, and all the other characters that were stuck at home were to be sent back inside the book thru the portal vortex. Angela found herself holding her father's hand as she walked into the living room. "Hey, mom! Look who we brought back home!" exclaimed Angela, who was still holding her father's hand.

As for the Ferraris, they are reunited and are back at home, but can they really still be happy knowing only the safety of the axe will keep the book closed, forever?

ABOUT THE AUTHOR

Sarah Amelia Tse was born on July15, 2003. She started writing stories when she was only 5 years old. The stories she writes about are of superheroes and their friends. Today she still writes stories and is now 11 years old , with a 4 year old brother named Jeremy Ryan whom she likes to play with.

Sarah's favorite hobbies are playing videos, hanging out and having adventures with cousins and friends. Her favorite foods are steak, ham, ice cream and cookies. The games she loves to play are Minecraft and her 3DS XL. Sarah currently is a 6th grade student at Cunningham, JHS.

www.ingramcontent.com/pod-product-compliance
Lightning Source LLC
Chambersburg PA
CBHW041030170626
46815CB00001B/32